The Lost Gardens

Written by Philip Osment
Illustrated by Michael Foreman

CHARACTERS

Old Lady

Maya

Jack

Emmy

Alice

Clifford

Albert

THE LOST GARDENS

(The play is set in a restored garden at the beginning of the 21st century, and in the same garden at the beginning of the 20th century.)

SCENE 1

(An Old Lady sits sleeping in a wheelchair.)
(sound effect: birds singing)

MAYA: *(offstage)* Jack! Through here.

JACK: *(offstage)* Where are you?

MAYA: *(offstage)* Over here.

(Maya enters and sees the Old Lady.)

OLD LADY: *(waking)* Ahhhh! There you are at last.

MAYA: Pardon?

OLD LADY: I've been waiting for you. Where are your friends? Jack and Emmy? Do you like the gardens? You know in the old days there were plants from all over the world here. People used to come especially to look at them.

MAYA: Yes, Miss Dickinson told us.

OLD LADY: But then the gardeners left and the family who owned the house moved away and the gardens were forgotten.

(Jack enters holding a map of the gardens.)

JACK: I think we've lost her.

OLD LADY: Ah, there you are, Jack.

(Jack looks up, surprised.)

MAYA: How do you know our names?

OLD LADY: I know everything. You're here with your school to look at the lost gardens. Now isn't it time you went and found the tropical garden?

JACK: What tropical garden?

OLD LADY: It's through there.

JACK: It's not on the map.

OLD LADY: That's because it hasn't been found yet.

(Emmy enters.)

EMMY: You're in trouble. We're not supposed to go off on our own.

OLD LADY: Ah, here she is.

EMMY: Who's she?

(The other two shrug.)

EMMY: She must live in the big house. It's a home for old people. Miss Dickinson said. She looks ancient.

MAYA: That's rude.

OLD LADY: That's all right, my dear. You're having a difficult time at the moment, aren't you, Emmy? Anyway I *am* ancient. It's true. Now the tropical garden's waiting for you. It's just the other side of the brambles. It used to be called the jungle.

EMMY: Cool.

JACK: It's not on the map.

OLD LADY: Where's your spirit of adventure? Now, you'll need this. There's a gate.

(She hands Jack a huge rusty key.)

OLD LADY: Go on. Take it.

(Jack takes it.)

OLD LADY: It's that way.

JACK: Thanks. Come on, Maya.

MAYA: Goodbye.

(Jack and Maya start to go.)

OLD LADY: But you can't leave without Emmy.

JACK: Oh … well …

OLD LADY: Yes?

MAYA: She doesn't really like the same games as us.

EMMY: Yes I do.

OLD LADY: Take her with you.

EMMY: I don't want to spoil their fun.

OLD LADY: You have to stay together.

(Jack looks at Maya. She shrugs.)

JACK: OK. Come on, Emmy.

OLD LADY: Goodbye, my dears. Be careful of the brambles.

(They go. The Old Lady sleeps.)

SCENE 2

(The children are crawling through brambles towards the gate.)

JACK: Aowhh, it's got my coat. Aowhh.

EMMY: Crybaby.

JACK: It's torn. My mum'll go crazy.

EMMY: Come on, I can see the gate.

(Emmy crawls towards the gate.)

MAYA: *(to Jack)* Shall we go back?

JACK: We can't just leave her.

MAYA: Why not?

JACK: My mum says we should be nice to her. Her dad went away to fight in the war. When he came back he was ill.

MAYA: But she's mean.

EMMY: Come on, you two, I need the key.

JACK: *(to Maya)* It might be fun.

(Jack crawls towards the gate. Maya follows him reluctantly.)

EMMY: Give me the key!

JACK: I'll do it.

(He puts the key in the lock, turns it and pushes open the door.)

SCENE 3

(The children step through to another time. It's 1912. The garden has palm trees and tropical plants.)

JACK: Wow, it really is like a jungle.

(sound effect: a parakeet)

MAYA: What was that?

JACK: Don't know.

(Maya looks for the gate.)

MAYA: Jack! Where's the gate?

JACK: It's just –

(He sees that the door in the wall has disappeared. Emmy's still looking at the trees.)

JACK: Emmy! The gate's gone.

EMMY: Don't be ridiculous.

(She tries to find the gate.)

EMMY: But it was – It's –

MAYA and JACK: It's gone.

(Alice enters through the trees. She's dressed in clothes of 1912. She's ten years old.)

ALICE: Hello.

(The three children jump.)

ALICE: Are you from Tasmania?

JACK: What?

ALICE: Did Papa bring you back from his travels? He's just come back from Tasmania.

MAYA: No. We're here with our school. I'm Maya. This is Jack. That's Emmy.

ALICE: You go to school?

MAYA: Yes.

ALICE: You're so lucky. I've just got Fräulein Bergmann. She's my governess. I wish I could go to school with other children. I'm Alice by the way.

MAYA: You have lessons on your own?

ALICE: Of course. Do you want to go and see the giant tree ferns? Mr Willis and the other gardeners are just planting them. Papa brought them back from Tasmania.

11

EMMY: Where's the gate gone?

ALICE: Pardon?

EMMY: There was a gate, there in the wall.

ALICE: Were you imagining it? I sometimes imagine things. Papa does want to put a gate there so we can come through here from the main garden. But he hasn't done it yet.

(Clifford comes running on. He's 13 years old.)

CLIFFORD: Alice! Fräulein says you have to do your Latin prep.

ALICE: Oh fiddlesticks.

CLIFFORD: And Mama says you're not to come out pestering Albert. He can't be your friend, you know. He's just a gardener – a servant. Mama says you shouldn't get friendly with the servants.

ALICE: *(to Maya, Jack and Emmy)* This is my brother, Clifford. He's a bit of a prig.

CLIFFORD: Alice Trevellion, I am not a pri– Who are you talking to?

ALICE: Well, this is Maya, and this is Jack and that's Emmy. They're here from their school.

CLIFFORD: Fräulein says you're to stop that, Alice.

ALICE: Stop what?

CLIFFORD: Making up imaginary friends.

ALICE: Can't you see them?

CLIFFORD: Walk through the wall, did they?

ALICE: They did actually.

EMMY: No we didn't. We came through the gate.

ALICE: You really can't see them?

CLIFFORD: You're insane, Alice.

(*Albert enters. He's 15 years old. He has a flower.*)

ALBERT: I brought you a camellia, Miss Alice.

ALICE: Oh thank you. Albert, can you see them?

ALBERT: See who?

ALICE: My friends. They're there.

ALBERT: Ah yes, now you come to mention it. How do you do?

JACK: How do you do?

CLIFFORD: Don't encourage her, Albert.

ALBERT: Sorry, Master Clifford. There are tadpoles in the pond, Miss Alice. I'll get some in a jar for you if you like.

CLIFFORD: You're supposed to be planting the new tree ferns.

ALBERT: Mr Willis told me to have my lunch.

CLIFFORD: Why aren't you having it then? Don't forget your prep, Alice.

(Clifford goes.)

ALICE: Why's he so horrible to you? You used to be friends.

ALBERT: It's since he went away to school. He came back in the holidays and he'd changed.

ALICE: Mama says school will make a man of him. My friends go to school.

ALBERT: Do they?

ALICE: Can you really see them, Albert?

ALBERT: No, Miss Alice. But I'm sure they're there.

EMMY: Of course we are.

ALICE: I wish I could go to school with other children. I hate having a governess.

ALBERT: Well she might be leaving soon.

ALICE: Why?

ALBERT: Because she's German. Mr Willis says that soon we'll be at war with Germany. And she'll be an enemy alien. They'll send her packing.

ALICE: I wouldn't want anything bad to happen to her.

ALBERT: If there's a war, all the gardeners will go and fight.

ALICE: Will *you* have to go and fight?

ALBERT: When I'm old enough. It's my patriotic duty.

ALICE: What's patriotic?

ALBERT: It means you love your country.

ALICE: I love Papa and Mama – well, sometimes – and Clifford I suppose. But I don't know how to love a whole country.

ALBERT: If you don't love your country, you're a traitor.

(Clifford enters.)

CLIFFORD: Alice, Mama's really cross. She says you won't have any lunch if you don't go and do your Latin prep.

ALICE: Oh, all right. *(to Jack, Maya and Emmy)* Will you still be here when I get back?

MAYA: I don't know.

ALICE: I hope so. Bye, Albert.

(Alice goes.)

CLIFFORD: Mad. Completely mad.

ALBERT: Maybe.

CLIFFORD: I wish I was old enough to go to war.

ALBERT: Eavesdropping were you?

CLIFFORD: What if I was?

ALBERT: Master Clifford –

CLIFFORD: What?

ALBERT: I'd like us to still be friends.

CLIFFORD: You're friends with Alice now. You have such a jolly time together while I'm away at school.

ALBERT: I don't have much time for jolly times between the weeding and the mowing and the planting.

CLIFFORD: You don't have time for me, you mean.

ALBERT: You want to come out with the ferret later on? Mr Willis says the rabbits are eating the vegetables and we have to catch them. Make a stew with them.

CLIFFORD: Mama says I'm not allowed.

ALBERT: Please yourself. No doubt you're too high and mighty now that you're a young gentleman.

CLIFFORD: You're supposed to take your cap off when you speak to me.

ALBERT: *(taking off his cap)* Sorry, Master.

CLIFFORD: And keep a civil tongue in your mouth.

(Jack, Emmy and Maya are shocked.)

ALBERT: Good day, Master.

(Albert goes.)

CLIFFORD: *(calling after him)* Albert! I didn't mean it.

(Clifford runs after him.)

JACK: *(to Emmy)* He's just like you.

EMMY: What?

JACK: He wants to be friends but he doesn't know how to be.

EMMY: No he's not. Sometimes people are your friend, and then they decide not to be your friend any more, and they find another friend and they don't want to be with you any more.

JACK: But Albert still wants to be friends.

EMMY: Albert's got Alice, he doesn't need Clifford.

MAYA: Should we go and find Miss Dickinson and the others?

EMMY: I want to stay here forever.

MAYA: We can't. My mum and dad and nan will be worried about me.

EMMY: They'll get over it.

JACK: Won't your mum miss you?

EMMY: She hardly knows I'm there half the time.

MAYA: Is it because your dad's ill and she's too worried about that?

EMMY: *(snapping)* Who told you that?

MAYA: Jack.

EMMY: You should both mind your own business. There's a hedge over there. I'm going to go through and see what's on the other side. Coming, Jack?

(Emmy leaves, squeezing through a gap in the hedge.)

JACK: *(to Maya)* We'd better follow her.

(Maya sighs and they both leave through the hedge.)

SCENE 4

(Emmy, Jack and Maya come through the hedge. It's January 1915.)

EMMY: Snow!

JACK: But it's the middle of summer.

EMMY: Not any more it isn't.

JACK: Do you think it's to do with global warming?

MAYA: Perhaps it's not real.

EMMY: Does this feel real?

(Emmy throws a snowball at Jack.)

JACK: Get off.

(Jack chases her with a snowball.)

EMMY: Ahhhhh! Get him, Maya.

(Maya goes to pick up a snowball. Alice enters. She's now 12 years old.)

EMMY: Hey, Alice! Snow!

ALICE: You've come back!

EMMY: We haven't been anywhere. Well, only on the other side of that hedge, with you.

ALICE: I always hoped you'd come back but you never did. I thought I'd never see you again. You look exactly the same.

MAYA: We are the same.

ALICE: Still wearing the same funny clothes.

EMMY: You can talk!

ALICE: It must be two years! I was only ten then. I'm 12 now! Why have you come back today? Is it because of Albert?

JACK: Albert?

ALICE: He's leaving for the war.

(Albert enters dressed in a soldier's uniform of 1915. He's now 18.)

ALBERT: Who are you talking to?

ALICE: *(embarrassed)* No one.

ALBERT: Imaginary friends?

ALICE: No.

ALBERT: You haven't seen any for so long now.

ALICE: I'm not a little child any more.

ALBERT: You cross with me?

(Alice looks away.)

ALBERT: I told you I'd have to go. When kings go to war then people like us have to suffer.

MAYA: Is he going to die?

ALICE: *(to Maya)* Don't say that!

ALBERT: Sorry. It's what my dad says.

EMMY: Not everyone who goes to war dies.

JACK: I think I recognise that uniform. Don't let him go, Alice.

MAYA: Why not?

(Clifford enters. He's now 16.)

CLIFFORD: So, you're off?

ALBERT: Yes. I'm getting the train at 2 o'clock. I'll be in France tomorrow.

EMMY: France? I thought he was fighting the Germans.

JACK: He is. The Germans invaded France, so the war happened there.

CLIFFORD: I hope it doesn't end before I'm old enough to join up. Just another two years.

ALBERT: They said it was going to be over by Christmas. It's January now and it's not over. I should be going.

JACK: Stop him, Alice. Don't let him go.

ALICE: *(looking at Jack and then Albert)* Please don't go, we'll hide you. I don't want you to go.

(Alice grabs Albert's arm.)

ALBERT: Stop it, Alice, I have to.

ALICE: Please, Albert, listen to me – you have to stay, it's too dangerous.

JACK: Stop him, Alice.

ALBERT: *(firmly)* Goodbye, Alice. Goodbye, Master Clifford.

CLIFFORD: I'll see you in France.

ALBERT: You'll be an officer. You won't be talking to the likes of me.

CLIFFORD: Goodbye, Albert.

JACK: Stop him, somebody.

(Albert goes. Alice sobs.)

CLIFFORD: Pull yourself together, Alice. He's just a garden boy.

ALICE: He's my friend.

CLIFFORD: Anyone would think you were sweet on him. Mama would have kittens. She's planning on you marrying Percy Reardon Smith.

ALICE: Be quiet, Clifford.

(Clifford turns and goes.)

MAYA: He'll come back. Tell her, Jack.

ALICE: *(drying her eyes)* Why did you want me to stop him?

JACK: What year is this, Alice?

ALICE: Don't you know? It's 1915.

JACK: Yes. I thought so.

EMMY: Wow! Cool!

JACK: It's the time of the First World War.

ALICE: The first? Are there more?

JACK: My mum took me to an exhibition where you could see what it was like to be a soldier at that time. They lived in trenches and they called it the Great War.

MAYA: What's great about a war?

ALICE: Are you from the future?

JACK: I think we are.

ALICE: So do you know what's going to happen?

(Jack says nothing.)

ALICE: How long is it going to last?

(sound effect: a train)

ALICE: There's his train. I must wave to him. Don't go away! I want to know when Albert will be back.

(Alice runs off to wave to the train.)

MAYA: Is it the war that we did in class?

EMMY: That was the Second World War.

JACK: The First World War was from 1914 to 1918.

MAYA: So Clifford will go and fight too.

JACK: More than 15 million people were killed.

MAYA: We have to tell her to stop him going.

EMMY: You think she'll listen to you? What do you know about anything? You don't know what it's like to have somebody go to fight in a war.

JACK: Stop it, Emmy.

EMMY: Why do you always take her side? I wish she'd never come to our school. You were my friend before she came.

MAYA: You shouldn't be so horrible.

EMMY: Why don't you just go back to Miss Dickinson? I thought you were worried about your mummy missing you.

MAYA: At least she *will* miss me.

JACK: Stop it, both of you. We've got to do something. We have to find Alice. It might not be too late to save Clifford.

MAYA: Can't we go somewhere warmer?

EMMY: She went that way through that archway.

(sound effect: a train)

EMMY: There's the train. Come on. What are you waiting for?

(They leave through the archway.)

SCENE 5

(The children appear through the archway.)

EMMY: Now it's raining.

JACK: She must be here somewhere. Alice!

MAYA: Alice!

EMMY: Look!

(Out of the mist walks Albert. He's now 19. He's shell-shocked and home on leave. It's autumn 1916. He has a bunch of flowers in his hand.)

MAYA: I thought he was meant to be going to France.

JACK: I think we've moved forward in time again.

EMMY: He's come back, hasn't he? He's been fighting. You can see it in his eyes.

(Albert turns and starts tearing the petals off the flowers.)

MAYA: What's wrong with him?

JACK: He's probably got that thing that soldiers get. What's it called, Emmy? Post something.

EMMY: Post traumatic stress disorder.

MAYA: Is that what your dad's got?

EMMY: Be quiet.

(Albert starts to whimper. He cowers and covers his ears with his hands. Alice enters with an umbrella. She's 14.)

ALICE: Albert? *(seeing Maya, Emmy and Jack)* Oh, you again.

JACK: Hello, Alice. Has it been long?

ALICE: You disappeared. Twice you disappeared. I needed you to tell me what would happen.

JACK: I'm sorry. How long has it been?

ALICE: I'm 14 now.

MAYA: What's happened to Albert?

ALICE: He has shell shock. He's been staying up at the house. Papa's letting them use it as a hospital for wounded soldiers. Albert, you have to come back to the house.

EMMY: I hate hospitals.

ALICE: Some of them have lost legs and arms. There's one that's all bandaged up and you can't see him at all. And some of them look all right but they're like Albert. The noise of the guns and the shells dropping has made them so ill that they can't stop shaking and they think they can still hear them even though they're back in England.

ALBERT: *(to Alice)* Talking to your friends? I talk to my friend. He died.

ALICE: Albert, you have to go back in, Dr MacKenzie wants to examine you.

ALBERT: He says I'll be able to go back soon.

MAYA: No. Tell her, Jack. Tell her how many people died.

ALICE: You can't go back, Albert. Not ever.

(Clifford enters wearing a raincoat. He's 17.)

CLIFFORD: Albert, they want you back at the house. The psychiatrist is here.

MAYA: Psychiatrist? Is he mad?

ALICE: No, he's not mad. He's ill.

CLIFFORD: I know, Alice, but it might help *(whispers)* you know, with the nightmares and stuff, before he goes back. *(To Albert)* Come on, Albert. They need to see if you're better.

ALICE: Anyone can see that he's not.

CLIFFORD: Everyone has to do their bit to defeat the Germans. Anyone who doesn't is a coward.

ALICE: Albert isn't a coward. He carried the body of his friend 300 yards while he was being shot at.

CLIFFORD: He was doing his duty. When I go out there next year, I'll do the same. Now come on, old boy. Let's be having you.

(Clifford starts to help Albert up.)

MAYA: Jack, tell her.

JACK: He'll have to live in the mud with shells falling all around him. And he'll have to climb out of the trench and run at the German lines while they're shooting at him with machine guns – just to gain a few feet.

ALBERT: Goodbye, Miss Alice. I picked you some flowers.

MAYA: Stop him, Alice.

ALICE: Tell them you're still sick, Albert.

ALBERT: I'm not a coward, Miss.

CLIFFORD: That's the spirit.

(Clifford and Albert go.)

ALICE: What are you three looking at? He'll be all right!

EMMY: No he won't. Everyone who goes to war gets hurt. Even the ones who don't get wounded. My dad promised me he'd come back. But when he did, it wasn't him. He was somebody else. He used to laugh. He never laughs any more.

ALICE: Did he go to war?

EMMY: Yes.

ALICE: You still have wars in the future?

EMMY: Yes.

ALICE: This is supposed to be the war to end all wars.

JACK: Alice, you have to think about Clifford. It's terrible over there.

ALICE: Do you think I don't know what's happening? I know that it's terrible. But there's nothing I can do. Nothing.

(Alice goes.)

JACK: Alice! Come back.

(Jack follows her offstage.)

MAYA: I'm sorry about your dad, Emmy. Will he get better?

EMMY: I don't know. I'm scared of him.

(sound effect: thunder)

(Jack returns.)

JACK: Come on, you two, she's gone through that gap in the fence, we have to go after her, we have to stop Clifford going to war.

(They leave through the gap in the fence.)

SCENE 6

(Jack, Emmy and Maya emerge through the gap in the fence. They're on a lawn.)

MAYA: There she is, look. She's really grown up. Alice!

(Alice walks on with a parasol. It's the summer of 1918 and she's 16. She ignores them and walks up and down looking at her watch.)

JACK: She can't see us.

MAYA: Alice!

(Maya tries to attract Alice's attention but fails. Clifford enters. He's now 19. He's dressed as an officer and is carrying his kit bag.)

JACK: Look! There's Clifford. He must have gone to the war.

ALICE: There you are! I heard the train ages ago. What have you been doing?

CLIFFORD: I had to go and see someone first.

(Alice and Clifford hug.)

ALICE: I've been so worried about you. How long have you got?

CLIFFORD: Just a few hours. I'll have to get the 3 o'clock train back to Southampton.

ALICE: I'd better take you straight to Papa. He's down by the wall. They're putting a gate in at last between the jungle and the vegetable gardens for the nurses to use.

CLIFFORD: It's all looking a little overgrown.

ALICE: Papa has to do everything himself now that there are no gardeners.

CLIFFORD: I hope he's not working too hard.

ALICE: It takes his mind off things. Come on, we should go and find him.

CLIFFORD: Wait!

(Alice stops and looks at him.)

ALICE: What is it?

CLIFFORD: Albert.

(Alice puts her hand to her mouth.)

ALICE: No!

CLIFFORD: They gave me leave to come and tell his parents. That's where I've just been.

ALICE: How?

(Clifford's reluctant to talk. Maya, Jack and Emmy come closer to listen.)

ALICE: Tell me, Clifford. I'm not a child any more.

CLIFFORD: When he went back to France he was never the same again. The nightmares, you know? One day they picked him up way behind the lines. On the road to Dieppe. They said he'd deserted.

ALICE: What did he say?

CLIFFORD: He said he was trying to come back to the garden.

ALICE: So what happened to him?

CLIFFORD: He was court-martialled, and found guilty of desertion.

ALICE: But he was ill.

CLIFFORD: Discipline has to be maintained. If men start running away then it's the men on the front line who suffer. They said he was a traitor. He was shot at dawn three days ago.

MAYA: No!

ALICE: *(shouting)* Why didn't you do something?

CLIFFORD: There was nothing I could do.

(Jack, Emmy and Maya are upset. Jack moves in to talk to Alice.)

JACK: Alice, I'm sorry.

ALICE: I don't want you here now. What good has it done meeting you? It hasn't changed anything. Go away!

(Jack backs away. Clifford watches her for a moment, knowing that she is seeing her "imaginary" friends.)

CLIFFORD: Alice, I promised to bring you a letter he wrote to you. I did that.

(Clifford takes the letter from his pocket.)

ALICE: Not good enough.

CLIFFORD: They were the rules, Alice.

ALICE: The rules are wrong. There must have been something you could have done.

CLIFFORD: I'd better go and see Papa. Are you coming?

ALICE: Who's the traitor? Albert for trying to get away from the guns? Or you for not saving your friend?

(Alice starts to go.)

CLIFFORD: Don't you want his letter?

ALICE: No. Not just to make you feel better.

(Alice goes. Clifford stands for a moment.)

CLIFFORD: Are you there?

(Maya, Jack and Emmy look at him.)

CLIFFORD: I know you're there. Look after it for her. Perhaps one day she'll want it. Will you?

(He puts the letter down on the ground.)

CLIFFORD: And look after Alice too. In case I don't come back. She could do with all the friends she can get right now, real or not. I'm so scared. So, so scared.

(Clifford turns and goes.)

EMMY: Shall I open it?

MAYA: No. We should keep it for her.

JACK: Did you hear what she said about the gate?

EMMY: What about it?

JACK: Now that it's been built maybe we'll be able to get back to our time.

MAYA: But what about Alice? We can't just leave her.

EMMY: Agreed. Come on, Jack, she went that way.

MAYA: Through those bushes.

(Emmy and Maya smile at each other and head through the bushes, followed by Jack.)

SCENE 7

(Jack, Emmy and Maya come through the bushes and are back in the jungle where they started. Alice is standing in front of the gate. She looks grown up. It's 1919. She's dressed for travelling.)

ALICE: Hello. I thought I might see you today. I wanted to see you one last time.

MAYA: Last time?

ALICE: We're leaving. I'm going to school in Switzerland and Papa and Mama are going to live in southern France.

MAYA: Won't that be dangerous with the war going on?

ALICE: Oh no, the war's been over for a year now.

MAYA: Is Clifford going to live in France?

ALICE: Clifford? Clifford was killed in the last week of the war. He was trying to rescue one of his men who was wounded and a sniper shot him just as he got back to his own lines. They gave him a medal.

MAYA: I'm so sorry.

ALICE: Mama says Papa will never get over it. He hasn't been in the garden at all since we heard the news. He just sits in the library looking out of the window. She hopes if they go somewhere else he won't be reminded of Clifford all the time.

EMMY: What about you?

ALICE: Mama wants me to marry Percy Reardon Smith after I finish school in Switzerland. She says there aren't many men left, so beggars can't be choosers.

EMMY: Do you want to read Albert's letter now?

(Emmy holds out the letter. Alice hesitates.)

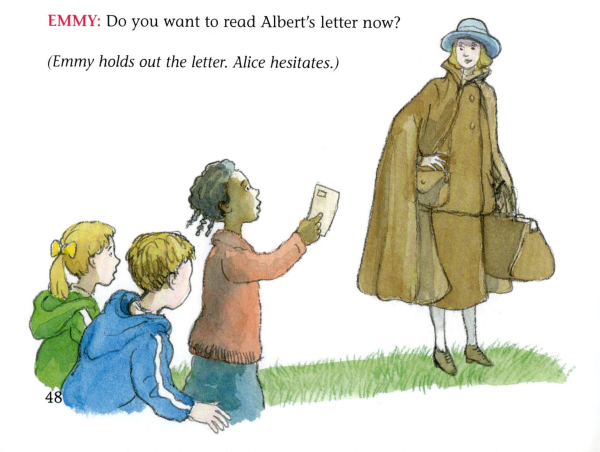

ALICE: I need to forget Albert. I don't want to spend the rest of my life thinking about what might have been. Now the taxi is coming. I have to lock the gate.

JACK: We can lock it.

(Jack holds up the key.)

ALICE: Where did you get that?

JACK: It's a long story.

EMMY: We don't have to go if you want us to stay with you.

ALICE: It's all right. I'm an adult now and adults can't go around seeing imaginary friends.

MAYA: We promised Clifford we'd look after you.

ALICE: I'll be all right. My whole life is before me. Mama says you have to remember that everything passes. When you think you can't bear it any more, you have to remember that it will change and that good things will happen again. One day I'll laugh again, she says. What do you think, Emmy?

EMMY: I want to go home and see my dad.

ALICE: Maybe one day he'll laugh again.

(sound effect: a car hooter)

ALICE: There's our taxi. Goodbye.

(Alice leaves.)

JACK: *(holding up the key)* Right. Here we go.

(They step through the gate.)

SCENE 8

(The Old Lady is sleeping in her wheelchair. Maya, Emmy and Jack enter.)

JACK: She's still here.

OLD LADY: Ah, you're back.

JACK: Yes. *(handing her the key)* Here.

OLD LADY: Thank you.

MAYA: Are they looking for us?

OLD LADY: They've probably not missed you. You've only been gone a few minutes.

JACK: No, we … but …

OLD LADY: Look at my watch, Jack.

(She shows him the time. Jack is puzzled.)

OLD LADY: So I believe you have something for me.

MAYA: Something for you?

OLD LADY: I've waited 90 years for this.

JACK: For what?

OLD LADY: Albert's letter! Don't you have it?

EMMY: You're Alice?

OLD LADY: So many times I wished I'd taken that letter.

(Emmy takes out the letter and hands it to the Old Lady.)

OLD LADY: Thank you, my dear. One thing I was right about. Things do change. I had a happy life in spite of everything. And now I'm back here living where I lived as a child. Of course it was sold and no one bothered with Papa's garden for nearly 90 years. Now they've rediscovered it and the house has been converted into a residential care home. They gave me my old bedroom – isn't that kind? It's like the time in-between was a dream and what's real now are the things that happened all those years ago.

JACK: Aren't you going to read the letter?

OLD LADY: Yes. When you've gone. It's private, you know. Hadn't you better go and find the rest of your class?

JACK: Yes, I suppose so. Goodbye.

(Jack and Maya start to go, then stop to look for Emmy who's still with the Old Lady.)

MAYA: Come on, Emmy. We're not going without you.

OLD LADY: *(to Emmy)* Goodbye, my dear. And remember, things do change.

EMMY: *(smiling)* Yes, I know.

(Jack, Emmy and Maya leave together. The Old Lady opens the letter. She smiles as she reads.)

Albert's diary

January 1915

Tomorrow I leave the Trevellion family and their beautiful gardens, and set off for France to fight in the war. I know a lot of other gardeners have signed up as well, and we're nervous but excited – we have a chance to do our patriotic duty and help to protect our country.

September 1915

Being in this war is more difficult than I'd expected. I knew people would die and I'd sometimes feel homesick, but I'd not expected to have so many nightmares, to see the horrors of the war even when I close my eyes.

October 1916

I'm home on leave now but I still hear the shelling of the trenches, and although I know I'm safe I can't stop myself from shaking. I keep thinking of my friend and how he died, even though I dragged him away from the bombs. I have to go back soon and I'm scared to go, but I'm not a coward. I have a duty to go. I have a duty to help protect this country.

April 1918

The nightmares keep coming. I spend all day seeing people hurt and then all night watching it repeating over again. I can't see a way it will ever end. If I can only get back to the garden for a bit, maybe the noise will stop. It used to be so quiet there, and so beautiful.

Ideas for reading

Written by Linda Pagett B.Ed(hons), M.Ed
Lecturer and Educational Consultant

Learning objectives: identify the ways spoken language varies according to context and purpose of its use; understand underlying themes, causes and points of view; improvise using a range of drama strategies; devise a performance considering how to adapt the performance for a specific audience

Curriculum links: History: How has life in Britain changed since 1948?; Citizenship: Children's rights – human rights

Interest words: civil tongue, court martialled, desertion, Fraülein, patriotic, prep, psychiatrist, Tasmania, tropical

Resources: writing materials

Getting started

This book can be read over two or more guided reading sessions.

- Ask one pupil to read the blurb to the others and ask the group to speculate what the play might entail. Prompt if necessary by drawing attention to the ghostly nature of one of the figures, and the soldier through the archway.
- Turn to p2 and introduce the characters, deciding who in the group will read each part. Scan the first scene together, identifying features of playscripts, e.g. sound effects.
- Ask children to think about how their part should be read, practising voice and tone.

Reading and responding

- Direct children to read the first scene together in their chosen parts. Discuss the effectiveness of this and encourage children to be supportive to each other's interpretation, e.g. *I like the way you ...*
- Put together a list of questions which the initial reading has prompted, e.g. How does the old lady seem to know so much?
- Ask children to read through the rest of the play in pairs, discussing their thoughts and predictions at the end of each scene.